THE L

"Richard O'Monroy" was the pen-name employed by Richard de L'Isle de Falcon de Saint-Geniès (1849-1916), a novelist and short story writer and one of the important storytellers of *fin-de-siècle* Parisian life. After graduating from the Saint-Cyr school in 1870, he became a cavalry captain, but in 1891 was forced to resign, which allowed him to devote himself fully to writing, a task which he did with unusual energy, eventually filling over fifty volumes with his tales.

RICHARD O'MONROY

THE LAST WALTZ
AND OTHER STORIES

THIS IS A SNUGGLY BOOK

Copyright © 2024 by Snuggly Books.
All rights reserved.

ISBN: 978-1-64525-157-6

CONTENTS

The Last Waltz / *9*
The Treatment / *16*
A Fatal Emotion / *23*
A Strange Tale / *31*
On Guard at La Belle-Épine / *39*
The Fugue / *50*
The Beauty Patch / *57*
The Violin / *66*
The Plebe that Turned / *73*
The Rehearsal / *84*
Mr. Jefferson's Advertisement / *94*
A Bear and a Brigadier / *102*
The Church Picture / *110*

THE LAST WALTZ
AND OTHER STORIES

THE LAST WALTZ

SHE lay dead in the little hotel in Budapest, and her face, although emaciated by disease, appeared again in all its classical beauty.

Upon her mouth there seemed to linger a sad, disillusioned smile; around her forehead, her hair, of a pale gold, fell abundantly upon the pillow in cascades, surrounding the pretty head like a halo of glory. But the closed eyelids hid the eyes—those immense eyes, larger than the mouth, it had been said. By looking into them one could have seen reflected there drowned people, in supplicating attitudes.

If the complexion had not formerly been white as pearl, as a water-lily, a ray of moonlight, dust of a butterfly's wing, one would have said only that she slept serenely.

At the foot of the bed a man was seated pensively upon a chair. In the distance was to be heard the Danube flowing under the iron bridge of old Ofen. The beautiful blue Danube! The rhythm so well known comes back to memory:

"Tra la la la-la la-la la."

And suddenly he saw again the past, the never-to-be-forgotten dinners, where, up high in the midst of flowers in his little balcony of the orchestra, above the door of the Restaurant Maillard, he literally poured down upon the convivial guests the beautiful music produced by his magic bow.

He was only one violin more, but his silence caused a loss to be felt in the orchestra. When he re-commenced, he made the melody appear grander and more beautiful, and the other musicians read his fantasy in his eyes by the movement of his fingers.

In the midst of a hurricane of shrill tones the clarinet sounded a piercing, discordant note.

In a languorous moment the violoncello gave forth the most thrilling strains, like skyrockets in the night, during which the cimbalom pearled indefinitely its crystal and aerial runs.

Ah! what success he had, what declarations were sent to him by the ladies who came there to take supper after the theater!

One night he was dazzled.

He saw a radiant fairy princess entering, covered with diamonds, draped in an immense opera cloak of mauve satin, dotted with gold, which showed her regal figure to perfection. Followed by a real court of friends, bearing illustrious names, and noted clubmen, she installed herself at a little table and became the center of attraction, exciting every one by her sparkling beauty.

And while she sipped the wine, her silvery laughter was heard falling like pearls, or her voice speaking to her neighbors with a pretty American accent, which reminded one of the caroling of a bird.

He had played for her, only for her, an old Tzigane melody; it was gay and joyous, merely a dance, but with features of inexpressible dignity, a heart-rending tenderness. Then, she had raised towards the balcony her beautiful eyes, as profound and as blue as the Danube; those large eyes, closed today, had looked at him, entranced, hypnotized, to such an extent that she gave no further attention to the jests of her merry companions.

After that she returned every evening regularly, towards the half-hour after midnight, drinking in his music, while looking at him in the golden balcony where he was king. Sometimes she toasted him discreetly with her glass of champagne. And thus things went on until the famous dinner, at the house of the Countess Palangridaine; a fatal dinner which decided everything. He had placed himself, with his musicians, in a boudoir, adjoining the dining-room, and had remained invisible during dinner, playing for the guests; but at dessert, by general request, he had come, with his violin, into the dining-hall, while his orchestra accompanied him in the distance. He had approached very closely to the princess and played for her "The Waltz of the Hero". In the innumerable arabesques of this delightful melody one could imagine the pawing of the ground by horses, the undulation of feathers, the clanking of sabers and spurs. The action was warm and decisive, and ended well for the hero, who returned singing. It was a joyous song, broken by the embracing of his comrades and the kisses of women.

This was too much for the princess. The next morning she deserted the conjugal nest, abandoning her husband, child, social position, everything, to follow him-to follow blindly the great conqueror—taking with her a box in which were thrown pell-mell her jewels and her dainty linen, embroidered with her family crest.

The dream had lasted barely two years. Sometimes the horizon looked dark for want of money, and now everything had come to an end. The princess was dead. Mechanically he took up his violin and began to play to the princess the waltz she had loved so much, as if by a miracle the rhythm could resuscitate her and bring her back to life. A far-away lamentation, like a sob suddenly strangled, then returning, long and desolate, ended with a shrill sound, dying again.

The attack upon the violin was startling: the chords twisted, tore and snapped; the teeth of a saw seemed to cut this beautiful instrument, bleeding and moaning with pain. And, by a strange hallucination, the flickering flame of the lamp caused shadows to appear at the corner of the pale lips of the dead princess, making them appear to smile at hearing this once much-loved waltz.

Suddenly a knock at the door was heard, and a messenger brought a telegram:

"A proposition is offered you to play upon the terrace, Hotel de Paris, during the week of the races at Trouville. Two hundred francs a night, and all found."

"Two hundred francs a night!"

In an instant the man was standing before the looking-glass, stroking his mustaches, and had resumed the victorious attitude of the balcony at the Restaurant Maillard. After looking himself over his conclusion was that his eye was just as black, his frame just as stalwart as at the time when he had won the princess. He would find again at Trouville all those great ladies; all those beautiful fools. Who could say but that the romance he had just lived might not be continued in a new chapter?

With a self-satisfied air, he took up a piece of paper and wrote:

"Hotel de Paris, Trouville. Accept—but make it two hundred and fifty. Place me well in sight—in the center of the terrace. I am going to order a beautiful new costume, old rose tights and shoes *à la* Ragotzky."

And, while the Danube continued to flow wrathfully in the distance, in the little room of the hotel in Budapest, the princess, stretching upon her bed, slept her eternal sleep, with her sad, disillusioned smile.

THE TREATMENT

THE VICOMTE TUGDUAL DE SAINT MONOKHL was surely not ill. A vigorous fellow who lived with his mother, the dowager Marquise, in their manor and spent his time in hunting, drinking, and making love to all the girls in surrounding towns. But since the last hunting season he felt ticklings in his throat, as if a small animal with a thousand feet took daily exercise there. They consulted Kerfauzon, their doctor. He declared that the Vicomte had granulations and needed a trip to Aix-les-Bains.

"They say it is a charming place," said the Vicomte.

"Is there a chapel?" asked the Marquise.

"Two superb churches!" said the doctor. "Besides, I know Doctor Lamiroux there. I will give your son a letter of introduction."

This is why Saint Monokhl landed at Aixles-Bains, with a collection of flannel suits with stripes not chosen for their vague hue. After getting settled at his hotel in a room with windows overlooking the lovely gardens, he presented himself at the house of Doctor Lamiroux, who was somewhat astonished to see enter his office that stout fellow with the figure of a major, the shoulders of a porter, and an anxious face.

"You have the rheumatism?"

"No, doctor, no; merely a tickling in my throat."

"Ah! Ah! Let us see that. Exactly. Very marked granulations. Lead to chronic catarrh."

"The devil! You alarm me. Chronic catarrh! A Saint Monokhl have it! It has never been known."

"But it can be stopped. I will prescribe, but you must follow my directions to the letter. Do you promise?"

"I swear to you on the head of Saint Tugdual, my patron!" said the Vicomte, solemnly.

The doctor wrote: "Every morning a sulphur bath, three-quarters of a glass of Challes water, half a glass at night. In the afternoon an hour of inhalation. For twenty-one days no late hours, no liquors, no dissipation, and one cigar after each meal—no more. I have your promise?"

"It is understood," said Tugdual, "and you know a Breton never breaks his word."

He carefully carried with him the doctor's writing and from that day he retired at midnight, wholly abandoned eau de vie, kummel, and chartreuse, lighted one cigar at the end of each meal, and lived quietly.

Certainly there was merit in it. Such charming women filled the hotels. All, all the most elegant, the most bewitching, and the greatest flirts. At night in the great hall, at dinner time it was a delightful sight, that show of dainty costumes around the small tables softly lighted by lamps with rosy shades. It was a grand symphony in white, a triumph of pale colors, with splashes of bright mauve, green, blue, and scarlet, clouds of festooned transparent stuffs, ruffles of lace, and bows of ribbon. Under white gowns petticoats of pink and lavender silk, black silk stockings embroidered in rose, or of white lace point d'Alencon inlaid with lilac. On the head, Directoire hats of white lawn or manilla straw, or the little Italian bonnet of lace and plumes. It was truly dazzling.

The Vicomte de Saint Monokhl—one might say, from this view, Saint Anthony—remained unmoved in the midst of all these temptations despite the luring glances from brilliant eyes. He had promised Dr. Lamiroux. He kept his promise. Each day a long walk, the unflinching swallowing of Challes water, the inhalation. Each day, after a meal without liquor, he lighted the cigar permitted by the doctor, disappeared a moment, returned looking rather pale, and, like a stoic, went off early to bed. When tempted to change one iota of his strict rules, he remembered his oath sworn by his saint, and the hideous catarrh.

With this rigid monastic life one would have thought the Vicomte might regain his superb health. On the contrary, he was visibly perishing. His cheeks wrinkled, his eyes were ringed with purple, in less than fifteen days he had lost half his weight, and the garments of beautiful striped flannel instead of outlining as before a powerful frame, hung from his shoulders in loose folds.

"Monsieur le Vicomte does not look well," said the hotel keeper, with interest. "Monsieur le Vicomte ought to marry and settle down. If I might be allowed to give respectful advice to Monsieur le Vicomte I would counsel rare steaks and cutlets and no more dissipation."

Strong in his conscience Tugdual made no reply, but he was forced to own to himself that something must be done. The dowager marquise would not have known him. He had lost all appetite and the sight of steaks and chops horrified him. He staggered as he walked and had fainting spells. He decided to visit Doctor Lamiroux.

"Heavens! how you have changed!" he could not keep from exclaiming at the sight of his patient.

"Is it not so, doctor, is it not so? It is necessary to tell you that for fifteen days I have not been able to keep my breakfast nor dinner. Nothing stays in my stomach. Nausea twice daily."

"The devil! That's a very bad sign. Ah! you have not followed my treatment then?"

"Yes, just because I had made you a solemn promise. But I knew very well, from the first day, that treatment would make me ill."

"Impossible! Perhaps—the inhalation—"

"No, I am quite used to it."

"It may be the Challes water. I own there is a certain scent—"

"No. I have grown to drink it with pleasure."

"I cannot believe that going without wine—"

"No, no, doctor, only you told me: One cigar after each meal."

"Well?"

"Well, your two damnable cigars are the cause of my not being able to keep breakfast or dinner since my arrival. I have obeyed, because I had sworn by Saint Tugdual, but—I have never in my life been able to smoke!"

A FATAL EMOTION

I never crossed the old bridge at Sommières without stopping at Père Langlade's confection stall. This was not because I still had a sweet tooth, but chiefly because of the presence of the pretty woman who sat by Langlade's side under a red umbrella.

She was his wife, Isaure; but while his red face and herculean build suggested a Marseilles porter, she, with her delicate and fragile beauty and her old-fashioned Artesian costume, which she wore with singular distinction, seemed like a princess who had become the victim of a strange *mésalliance*.

She was very pale, and there were little red spots on her cheeks. It was generally understood that her heart was affected.

All this aroused my interest, and as I bought my candy I sought to discover the secret of this queer mismating.

Langlade seemed to be a good fellow, rather vulgar, but he evidently adored his wife and paid her the tenderest attentions, which she accepted with a smile of sadness and resignation.

In the South people are friendly and love to talk, and so, after many small purchases, I came to be regarded as a friend as well as a customer.

Langlade asked my advice and followed it, and showed a flattering confidence in me.

The fair Isaure, however, remained shy and reserved, though her fine eyes would brighten when I spoke of Paris, the city of light, animation, noise, flowers and love.

As I crossed the bridge one morning I was surprised to find the booth closed.

The next day I found Langlade without the beautiful Arésienne.

"I do not see Madame Isaure," I said. "Is she ill?"

"Yes—a little. That wretched heart, you know. Ah!-!-! I am nothing but a brute!" exclaimed the colossus, thrusting his fingers through his shock of hair.

"Why, no! Not at all," I said. "I know you pretty well, and you are a very good fellow. You are not doing yourself justice."

He struck the table with his fist and made the candies jump. Then he said, in his deep bass, and with his chopping provincial accent:

"Listen, and then, for Heaven's sake, give me your honest opinion. You can judge whether I did right or wrong. I am an ignorant man, and I don't know—I don't know!"

I took the seat usually occupied by the fair Isaure, and he continued, in great excitement:

"I met her three years ago, at Arles, where I had gone to buy confections. When I saw Isaure, with her little black cap, her red silk *fichu* and her long earrings, I thought she had just dropped from heaven. She was very proud and high-toned and made me disgusted with the sort of women one finds here. I became crazy over her. For her part, I don't know if she loved me—one can never tell that—but she was sweet and kind, and always greeted me with a smile.

"To make a long story short, I married her. I had a little money saved up, and my business was good, so her parents had no objection. But her mother said, very seriously:

"'My lad, be careful with Isaure. You seem rather violent and easily angered. Isaure's heart is weak, and the doctor says the slightest emotion might be fatal. So no bad words, no quarrels! Only on that condition can you have our child.'

"Quarrels! Bad words! There was no fear of that, I loved her so.

"Ah, monsieur, I was as gentle as a lamb. I gave up drinking, I gave up smoking, I gave up swearing. I tried to soften my big voice for her pretty ears.

"It is not my fault that my hands are big and my fingers thick and clumsy, but I treated my wife like a precious vase that one is fearful of breaking. I was as timid with her as with a delicate child, she seemed so to need petting and protection.

"The doctor here examined her, and he, too, said she must be spared all violent emotions. Those red spots on her cheeks—you've noticed them, I suppose—well, it seems they meant that something might happen some day.

"Still our life was pleasant enough. I installed her in the chair where you are sitting, under the big red umbrella. There was always something to see, people crossing the bridge, carts, carriages, flocks of sheep—a continual going and coming.

"Business was brisk, too, and the day passed like a dream.

"Among our favorite customers—of course, I am not classing him with you, monsieur—was a brigadier of gendarmes named Rouflard, a married man, who often stopped to buy candies for his children.

"He was a dapper little chap, with his uniform always spick-and-span and his kipi cocked fiercely over his ear. It used to amuse

Isaure to play with the gold tassels of his epaulettes and hear them rattle on his chest.

"I noticed that she always gave him very good measure but, pshaw! he had children, and military men are not rich, so I shut my eyes.

"Besides, a man can't make himself over. My father, an old gamekeeper, had brought me up to respect shoulder-straps. Rouflard was a gendarme, that was enough. I had confidence in him.

"When he went to his post in the morning, while Isaure was still at home doing her bit of housework, he would cross the bridge without stopping, merely giving me a nod and a friendly 'Good morning.' But when he came off duty in the afternoon he had time to stop and have a little chat. Sitting on a bench, very straight and elegant, smoking a cigarette and daintily flicking off the ash, he would tell amusing stories to Isaure, who never took her eyes off him.

"And, blind that I was, I saw nothing —nothing!

"As the postman passed yesterday morning, he grinned and asked: 'Is the Missus at home?'

"'Yes,' said I. 'What of it?'

"He laughed.

"'She isn't lonely?'

"'What do you mean?'

"'Oh! Brigadier Rouflard is with her, that's all.'

"'You lie, you scoundrel!'

"'Very well. See for yourself. It's just the same every morning.'

"Great Heaven! The blood rushed to my eyes and everything turned red. Sometimes one doesn't reflect—isn't that so, monsieur?

"I left my booth and ran home. I went in like a shot, without knocking—and I found that the postman had told the truth!

"Roaflard, the coward, ran away and left me face to face with Isaure, who was deathly pale—white as a sheet.

"And seeing her so, I forgot everything, my anger, my thoughts of revenge, of murder—for I had even thought of that—and I had only one idea, that by my sudden entrance I was going to cause her the emotion, the fatal emotion, that I had so solemnly promised to shield her from. I fell on my knees.

"'Calm yourself, my darling,' I said. 'I beseech you, my love, do not worry about such a trifle.'

"And I made her drink some orange cordial.

"Still, you see, it gave the poor girl a terrible shock. Now, tell me frankly, monsieur, do you think I did wrong?"

I looked at the giant who had told me all this in a broken voice, and who was so honest, so naive in his loyalty, so sublime in his unconscious self-abnegation.

To many a man, no doubt, the poor candy seller would have seemed only ridiculous, but I confess that I was deeply moved.

I pressed his hand and said, very softly: "Père Langlade, you are a good man."

A STRANGE TALE

IT was at our last promotion dinner at the Military Circle. Of the old three hundred Saint Cyprians we were a hundred and sixty, some bearing themselves well and valiantly defending their maturity against the first attacks of age, others already bald, with protuberant abdomens, showing the head of the superior officer before the coming of the fourth stripe of gold lace. Of course, the conversation turned on those who had disappeared, the dead, with that "Don't you remember?" which is like a refrain to those banquets filled with recollections of the past. They talked of Julian killed at Bomy, of Brahaut, of Mezensac passing on horseback with erect trunk after a cannon-ball had carried off his head before the horrified squadrons.

The martyrology continued, a litany augmented each time by a new name of a hero. We were at the psychological moment, when, through the action of good wines and of digestion, one feels a heightened nervous sensibility producing a peculiar spiritual state.

"And d'Iramond," said Chavoye; "you recollect d'Iramond!"

Suddenly grave, Commander Fabert said:

"Gentlemen, I was then Captain of the Seventeenth Chasseurs, and I declare to you I cannot think of the affair without feeling the distress that seizes you before problems that our reason refuses to comprehend."

"Tell us the particulars! We want the details!" was the cry all around.

"Well, gentlemen, it was five years ago. We were then at Saint Germain, the most adorable of garrisons. Mornings in the forests, joyous breakfasts at mess, flirtations on the terrace, and at night the grand life of Paris. Captain d'Iramond, with his name, his great fortune, his elegance and graceful swagger, held his own brilliantly amid our mad revels, always the last at supper, and the first in the saddle.

"Suddenly everything changed. The Duchess d'Iramond died of aneurysm of the heart. From the moment when the Captain had no longer his mother, mamma, as he said with a filial tenderness, a touching contrast in the mouth of that big moustachioed boy, from the day when he could not go to her from time to time to recover from our dissipations, he was not himself. He ceased to go to Paris, and beyond the duties of the service he never left home, where he remained for hours before a portrait of the Duchess painted by Cabanel. He gazed upon the dear dead, with her blonde hair waved and worn in the style of the Empress Eugenie, her sweet smile, her blue eyes which seemed to gently follow him to every corner of the room. In vain I tried to drag the Captain from that fixed idea.

"'No,' he said, 'I have all at once become old, for as long as one has his mother one can believe himself young. Life flung to the winds each day is but a dream without those regular halts that one can make under the maternal roof, those times of pausing where one can take breath and examine his conscience. They are much to be pitied who have not a family corner to repose in, and to seek to regain strength and be more sure of one's self.'

"He became more and more taciturn and more and more concentrated in himself. One fine winter morning, going to his house on the way to the maneuver, I found him especially agitated.

"'You will laugh at me,' he said at once, 'but the most extraordinary adventure has happened to me.'

"'What was it?'

"'You know Father Yincent? Imagine my seeing him come this morning accompanied by a choir boy and bearing the Holy Sacrament. You may know I was astonished.

"'"You have made a mistake, monsieur, doubtless you are wrong in the address."

"'"No, no; I was told to go to the house of Captain d'Iramond."

"'"Then someone is indulging in an unbecoming joke, and I will know the author."

"'"Monsieur, I assure you that the lady who sent me to your house had the most respectable and trustworthy air."'

"'"A lady?"

"'"Yes, a lady whom I met on the square by the church—Ah! there she is!"

"'And Father Yincent showed me the portrait of mamma hanging on the wall. I own that I could not help feeling a tug at my heart.

"'"You are quite sure that this is the lady you met?"

"'"Yes, Captain—oh! I should recognize her amid a thousand others. She insisted so, with such a gentle and sad air. She said to me: 'Run quick! There is but just time!' Yes, yes, it is the lady of the portrait."

"'"But, monsieur, that picture—it is of my mother, the Duchess d'Iramond, scarcely two months dead."

"'The priest trembled, and turned a little pale, then he said:

"'"My dear son, the designs of Providence are impenetrable. Receive the viaticum. It is always a good thing to be at peace with God. And then—who knows—it would doubtless give pleasure up above to Madame, the Duchess."

"'Then I made no further objections; much affected I confessed and received the sacrament. Perhaps the priest had a hallucination; perhaps he had been swayed by a resemblance. Anyway, it is done, and now, forward, for the maneuver!'

"I remember that it was cold and dry like today. D'Iramond mounted a superb chestnut that he had bought the day previous. We went off at full trot to join the classes on the terrace, and the hard ground made a metallic noise under our horses' feet.

"I tried to joke with my friend to divert him, but he, very gloomy, always returned to the priest's visit, saying, in a strange voice: 'After all, you must own that it was queer.'

"We reached the squares, answered the roll-call, and joined our squadron. At that moment a recruit lost control of his horse and came charging upon us. The poor boy had completely lost his wits and thought of nothing but to cling to the pommel of his saddle. The shock was terrible. My army horse, an old stager used to such surprises, never flinched, but d'Iramond's chestnut, alarmed, bounded wildly and fell prostrate; in one second I saw a confused mass, a horse that after desperate struggles sprang up,—and on the ground my unfortunate friend, senseless, his skull broken by a blow from his horse's hoof. By a deplorable chance the doctor was not there. The wounded man was taken to Saint Germain in the sutler's wagon, and when at last he could be cared for, it was too late. He died that night at five o'clock without having uttered a word, without recovering consciousness, and I who knew the story of the priest, I insisted upon adding to the announcement of his death: *Provided with the Sacraments of the Church.* Now—if one were superstitious!"

There was a silence, then big Pouraille cried:

"The devil take you with your dance-of-death adventures that give the shudders! Do you want my conclusion? The priest was hired—D'Iramond liked to drink! Gentlemen, let us have coffee, and for the rest of the evening, for pity's sake let us talk only about the ladies, will you? Otherwise I shall have bad dreams."

ON GUARD AT LA BELLE-ÉPINE

OH! how bored I was that day!

It was during the second siege of Paris, and I had been placed with my squadron on guard at La Belle-Épine, six miles from Notre-Dame.

Poor Belle-Épine! Such a charming inn as it had been once upon a time—gay, noisy, lively, full of travelers, postillions, and pretty maid-servants.

Louis XV went there with Madame de Pompadour, and planted the tree which served as the inn's sign. Since then many other lovers had written their names on its bark, while they drank the little wine of the country in its shade.

Then one day silence had suddenly succeeded to noise, travelers and postillions had ceased coming, and the pretty maid-servants themselves had fled away, leaving the inn empty and deserted.

The Prussians were coming.

These latter had, of course, burnt up the doors and the furniture, broken the windows, stolen the old kitchen clock, and smashed in the roof. On the day on which we encamped there, there remained of La Belle-Épine only some blackened walls, behind which one could just find shelter from the shells which the Commune was sending out from Villejuif and Hautes-Bruyeres.

Before us the road to Italy stretched out indefinitely, white, dusty, flooded with sunlight. The orders were to let no one from Paris pass, and they were easy to carry out. Not a cart, not a man, not a dog broke the gloom of the landscape. Now and then a little white cloud rose above the paving-stones. On looking closer you saw that it was another projectile that had just burst. Only the day before we had had wonderful luck; a woman selling potatoes had tried to pass with her cart; as she appeared to be a suspicious character, she was ordered to turn back. She refused, and, in short, was arrested and sent to the General. This important event had certainly occupied fifteen minutes, and it was anyhow a distraction; but today no woman selling potatoes appeared on the horizon.

And my companions were in a dreadful temper. The Captain had just learned that the trousers that had accompanied him through the entire campaign of the Army of the Loire were not eternal, and showed their age by a large opening in the portion which touches the saddle. It was I who had timidly pointed this out to him, and I greatly feared the consequences of my perspicuity. The Lieutenant, who had expected to be married early in the Spring, was wondering whether the powers that be intended to keep him a bachelor much longer, and also overwhelm him with colds in the head, due to sleeping in the open air. To amuse himself, he was whistling a little air between his teeth, very much out of tune. There was also a second lieutenant, but he never said a word; he contented himself with smoking, and with blowing great clouds from his pipe at even intervals. Did he think about anything?—I don't know, but this mute smoking gave him an appearance of great profundity. If you spoke to him, he fixed you with a round impassive eye.

You thought he was about to answer,—two or three puffs of smoke issued from his mouth, and that was all,—he gravely continued to smoke.

These were the agreeable persons with whom the Commune forced me to spend my existence. On my way home from Germany, where I had been a prisoner for five months, I had, all through the journey, dreamed of Paris as one dreams of the promised land, and I had barely arrived when I was obliged to fight against the city which epitomized all the memories and all the joys of my youth. My thoughts were becoming gloomy. I reflected that I was ridiculous, and to cheer me up I went and tried to read the German verses written on the tombstone of a Prussian officer killed at Chevilly and buried behind the inn. I had abready deciphered the first line: *Ade liebe Bruder* "Fare well, beloved brother," when I was interrupted in my task by my three companions' cries of astonishment.

There was a black dot on the horizon towards Paris, a large black dot, advancing tranquilly through the little white clouds I have mentioned. We got an opera-glass; we passed it from eye to eye, and we soon unanimously decided that it was a vehicle, and actually a furniture truck! Who could the individual be who was sufficiently original to drive out in a furniture truck under the rain of bombs and shells which inundated the road?

The moment was certainly ill-chosen for such a journey. Once a projectile fell so close to the truck that we expected to see it pull up. It did not, however, but continued to approach.

When it got within a few steps of us the Captain, who had always declared that nothing could startle him, was unable to suppress a gesture of astonishment. In the front of the truck, seated on a red satin sofa and wrapped in a camel hair shawl, was a remarkably beautiful woman. She was fair, and pink, and smiling, and her large, blue eyes showed not the slightest emotion. Behind her were piled together pell-mell silk curtains, buhl cabinets inlaid with mother-of-pearl, rosewood tables, looking-glasses, bronzes, and all sorts of expensive furniture. A Japanese vase held a great, green plant, which waved its leaves over her head to protect her from the sun; and amid this confusion, with her calm face, she looked like a princess in a Chinese palace.

A man in a blouse was leading the horses by the bridle. He was covered with dirt from the shells, and his pallor contrasted with the placidity of the woman he was escorting.

When she reached us she gave the order to stop, and then bowed very prettily to the Captain.

"Good morning, Captain. I'm very glad to be among Christians at last. I'm like the snail, you see: I travel with my house on my back— through the bombs."

And she burst out laughing.

She was really charming, and I should never have guessed that so much pluck could be hidden under such a delicate exterior.

The Captain instinctively drew together the divorced portions of his trousers, and forced them to live together for the time being, then, reassured as to his prestige, he put on his most formidable voice, and with the pose of a gendarme examining a legal document, asked:

"Where do you come from? Where are you going?"

"Why, I come from Paris. It is no fun there any more! If you could see the boulevards! it's really sad; all my friends are gone and the theaters are all closed. The Communist staff officers are the swells just now, and they are so dirty! Such caps, such beards, such faces, it's ridiculous. If I had had to stay among that lot, I should have died. I have a little box of a house at Longjumeau, a regular little nest. Not very big, you know, but very pretty, and I am going there to wait for better days."

"There is only one obstacle to this plan, madam, which is, that I shall not allow you to pass."

She looked at the Captain in astonishment. Probably no man had ever dared to speak to her in such a tone before, and not understanding such a rough injunction, she looked about to see whether help was possibly to be found among the rest of us.

The Lieutenant looked at her indifferently, unenthusiastically, as one whose mind and thoughts were elsewhere. He was no ally.

Behind him was the Second Lieutenant; he was smoking with his usual impassiveness. Neither did his large, round eyes give promise of help.

I was in the background—and I admit that I was looking at her with all my eyes. I don't know whether she noticed this, but she raised her voice:

"What, you won't let me pass? Do you know that you are extremely impertinent, monsieur? Are you going to be as rude as the Communist commanding La Porte d'Italie?—a person whom I would not let into my stable for fear of soiling it, and who forced me to parley with him for half an hour. I was obliged to be polite and make the gentleman's conquest, and I finally tamed him so thoroughly that he insisted on treating me to a glass of horrible currant brandy."

"How disgusting!"

"Come! I am sure you are going to let me off cheaper!"

And she gave him a glance which would have softened a tiger.

The Captain never flinched, but replied: "Madam, when the orders are that no one is to pass, no one passes. If Madam Thiers herself was to appear, I should turn her back."

I am convinced that he was thinking of the advertising wood cut, in the shops, of *La Redingoie Grise*, which represents a conscript stopping Napoleon, and telling him he couldn't pass if he were the Little Corporal himself.

She looked at me again. This time I made a heroic resolve, and burned my bridges behind me. Time was precious and I had to force the situation. I came forward and pretended to suddenly recognize her.

"What! is that you? *you* here?" and climbing into the truck I fell into her arms and kissed her vigorously. How willingly I acted my comedy, and how natural I must have been in the part! She screamed, but I whispered: "Silence, and you'll get through."

You may imagine that a brave little woman who was not afraid of bursting shells was not going to faint because an officer of dragoons, whom she had never laid eyes on before, kissed her without warning. So she threw herself bravely into the part, and I felt two soft arms about my neck, while her lips touched my forehead.

I turned to the Captain, slightly upset.

"I have known this lady for years, and I can answer for her as for myself. I trust, Captain, that you will now allow her to pass, and will even give her an escort of ten dragoons. This will allow her to reach Longjumeau without further trouble, and will afford you, in addition, a means of verifying her identity."

The Captain, after much persuasion, agreed, and I feared for a moment that, for greater security, he intended to accompany the ten dragoons himself. Luckily, I reminded him in time that his trousers had been with the Army of the Loire. The Lieutenant would have been unwilling to compromise himself by appearing in company with such a good-looking person; the Second Lieutenant would have been obliged to stop smoking, which would have vexed him greatly; in short, the command of the escort was left to me.

I placed five dragoons in front of the truck and five behind, and I set forth in triumph with my prisoner.

※

She is snatching away my pen, and declaring that the rest of the story does not concern the public. And after all, she is perhaps right, for it is already ancient history.

THE FUGUE

WISHING to keep the national holiday in some out-of-the-way corner of Normandy, I was striding up and down the hall of the Saint Lazare Station when I heard an inharmonious feminine voice address me—inharmonious but feminine.

"M. Richard! M. Richard!"

I turned round. It was my friend Mme. Manchaballe, in a traveling costume consisting of an old surah dust-cloak, trimmed with black lace that had formerly done duty at Aix with Rebecca (I knew it again), and a Leghorn hat with a heap of flowers and two pink ibis wings. However vivid your imagination may be, I defy you to present to yourself Mme. Manchaballe's head adorned with two pink ibis wings. You ought to have seen it, for it is a never-to-be-forgotten spectacle.

"Where are you off to, my dear lady?"

"I'm going to join my youngest, Caroline, at Houlgate, where we have a little cottage on the Corniche."

"Caroline? Ah, yes! she goes in for singing. Well, are the Conservatory examinations over?"

"They're over," groaned Mme. Manchaballe; "they're over, but they never began for us."

"Impossible!"

"Oh, monsieur, a piece of flagrant injustice! We did not even enter for them. And yet Caroline has a nice voice. Don't you remember the evening she sang, from *Faust*:

> 'Ah, how I love to see myself look so nice in this mirror!'

and then the great recitative:

> 'I should much like to know who that young man was!
> If he is a great noble, and how much he gives——'"

"Those are not exactly the words, Mme. Manchaballe."

"Yes, but it's the meaning. In operas words are of no importance. Well, if you remember, you were surprised yourself, and cried, 'The deuce! Your daughter has made great progress. I will recommend her to my friend Victorien Sardou.'"

"Joncières, I said Joncières."

"Well, they're both Victorien, so where's the difference? I didn't let the grass grow under my feet. Not only did I give her lessons from Mme. Saxe, but I made her call on all the members of the jury without me. At first I wanted to go with her, but she said I made her nervous, and that she sang better when I wasn't there. So I did not insist."

"I think you were quite right, Mme. Manchaballe."

"Yes, yes. And, besides, I was busy. I went to the Concert Vatoire. A funny sort of concert, I must say! A queer room, half theater, half study. The stage, with its two chairs and one door, looked like a porter's lodge, and a poor porter too. Not a decoration, not a piece of furniture, not an ornament on the bare walls, which were painted the color of raw beef. It seems that this plain, bare background is good for judging gesture, pose, and play of feature. Well, I didn't mind. Instead of the usual boxes, there was a long table of severe aspect, behind which the members of the jury were seated, with the president in the center, all getting gray, short-sighted, and not handsome at all. Such beards, such heads of hair! Why do all musicians have such extraordinary heads of hair? Perhaps music is good for the hair."

"I think you are straying from the point, Mme. Manchaballe. I want to hear about Caroline."

"Just so, I'm coming to it. In short, one day I arrived late, at the end of the performance, and heard that Mlle. Terville had the first prize for her fugue, an unheard of fugue, an extraordinary fugue, a marvelous fugue, that literally carried the jury away. And all round me I heard the critics exclaiming, 'What a fugue! Ah, my dear fellow, what a magnificent fugue!' In order not to seem out of it, I said the same, smiling like the rest. But in fact—don't laugh at me—I hadn't the least idea what a fugue was. So far, with Judith and Rebecca, I have only had to do with dancing. With pirouettes and the like I was quite at home, but I had never heard a mention of fugues. So that as soon as I got out into the vestibule I went up to Mme. Chapuzot, Stella Chapuzot's mother, who was in the same class as Caroline—and Mme. Saxe had always said, 'If Stella doesn't make a success at the opera first, it will be Caroline.' Well, Mme. Chapuzot was very jealous of us. I ought to have been on my guard, but I thought all would be right between mothers. So I went up to her and said, 'Mlle. Terville had a great success with her fugue—that is to say, she's certain of the prize. And,' I went on, 'since I wasn't there, it would be very kind of you to tell me what a fugue is, because, you see, I'd make Caroline prepare one.'

"Then Mme. Chapuzot began to laugh, and so loudly that everybody turned round to look at us. I laughed, too, for company's sake, but without exactly knowing why. Suddenly Mme. Chapuzot became serious, and said, 'A fugue, Mme. Manchaballe, is to make yourself scarce just at the moment when it would be least expected. Suppose you are to sing in the evening at the Opéra Comique: at eight o'clock, precisely, you decamp to Italy. That's a fugue. Then the terrified directors, in order to bring you back, prefer either to increase your salary or to give you a prize. That is what was done in the case of Mlle. Terville.'

"I thought it rather extraordinary. But the same evening I met by chance at the opera one of our former tenants, M. Jules Claretie, who is a member of the Academy, and consequently understands the French language, and I said to him, 'M. Claretie, if a person had to sing at the Opéra Comique at half-past eight, and at eight decamped to Italy, would that be a fugue?'

'Certainly,' replied the Academician with perfect politeness, 'that would be a fugue.'

"I hesitated no longer. I waited for the day of the competition, and then hey presto! without a word of warning, I packed Caroline off to Houlgate. She objected, but I said, 'Leave everything to your mother; it's for your own good.' I went to the concert-hall, and when Caroline's name was called I stood up and said, 'She's doing a fugue. She's in her cottage at the seaside.'

"'Good,' replied the president.

"And he summoned the next, Stella Chapuzot. And she passed, and Caroline failed. Now, isn't it disgraceful, monsieur? I ought not to have trusted Mme. Chapuzot; but, honestly now, could I suspect M. Claretie? Such a distinguished man! Put it into the papers, will you? It will prove to the government that, say what they like, there's no equality yet; and that what spells success for one is fatal to another. But there's my train. Goodbye!"

"A pleasant journey to you, Mme. Manchaballe!"

THE BEAUTY PATCH

THE SAINT-LAZARE STATION is a gay station, in the heart of the city, a stone's throw from the Opera and the boulevard, five minutes from the Champs-Elysees, twenty minutes from the Bois de Boulogne. In the waiting-room, the Hall of the Lost Footsteps, lined up before the booking-offices or seeking *quem devorent*, there are always a lot of pretty girls, with extravagantly yellow hair crowned by marvelous hats. They walk down the Rue d'Amsterdam, their noses in the air, striking the echoing curbstones with their little high heels, and generally carrying small leather bags—supposed to give them a countenance.

What a countenance! Hence, trips to Saint-Germain or Versailles, starting from the above-mentioned gay station, are true pleasure trips.

Yesterday I was obliged to go to Versailles, and profiting by my experience—in garrison there for several years—I strolled up and down, in no haste to choose my compartment. The railway carriages standing high above the level of the platform, the women passengers have to practice regular gymnastics to get aboard, and there are, therefore, all sorts of picturesque sights to be seen, not to speak of services to be rendered. For the latter purpose, the best thing to do is to stand opposite the revolving platforms. They make the steps at least a foot higher—enough to make one quite dizzy climbing in. I was on the lookout for a pretty fellow-traveler. I might even say that I had the embarrassment of choosing; it almost looks as if the Western Company has the monopoly of good-looking ticket-holders. But alas! Not one of them was alone. Naturally, I avoided cavalry officers, they all go to the terminus of the line.

The infantry add to the chances of a tête-à-tête, for they generally get off at Courbevoie, Saint-Cloud, or Ville-d'Avray. As to the artillery—that's a risk to run; there is a battery at Suresnes, but there are two regiments at Versailles as well.

I was at this stage of perplexity when, in one of the last of the first-class compartments, I caught sight of a pretty brunette—to be classified among the piquant brunettes—velvety eyes, fringed with long lashes, a faintly shadowed upper lip, and above the left corner of the mouth—a souvenir of a by-gone century—a dainty little black patch that our gallant ancestors would have called killing. She wore a maize-colored bengaline bodice, trimmed with guipure; on her head was perched a big hat with outspread white wings, that made her look like a Valkyrie—but a gay, not a warlike one. Beside her was seated a large, elderly gentleman, with big mustaches, a decoration in his button-hole; he had a military air and imposing eyebrows, and was reading the paper.

But, from time to time, he raised suspicious eyes on her—the eyes of a proprietor defending his domain. The husband, evidently.

I got into the carriage, and seated myself discreetly opposite the pair, but in the far corner. Although I had made a slight bow on entering, I did not have the good fortune to claim the lady's attention; she seemed preoccupied, and kept her head out of the window, as if she were expecting someone. The mustached gentleman, however, returned my bow most politely. He was no doubt obliged to me for having left the seat opposite him unoccupied. At the moment the train was starting, a handsome, blond young fellow, carrying a briefcase under his arm, sprang inside breathlessly. He rapidly exchanged a smile of intelligence with the lady, and then sat down opposite her, knee to knee.

"Look sharp!" I said to myself. "This is going to turn out interesting."

Naturally, the big, elderly man, absorbed in his paper, had noticed nothing. The whistle sounded, the train started, and the fair young man, no doubt to appear occupied, began to turn the leaves of the voluminous document in the leather case. But every now and then he raised his eyes, and then it was easy to see that the lady with the patch smiled at him imperceptibly. It would have been impossible to be more imprudent, and this little maneuver, barely concealed, ran a great risk of being discovered by the man with the terrible eyebrows.

My soul is instinctively lenient to human weaknesses, and at the bottom of my heart I always find a secret pleasure on learning that the corporation of husbands counts one more victim. So, as far as was possible, I decided to come to the assistance of the sweethearts by attracting the attention of the husband. Seizing the first slight pretext, I engaged him in conversation. As we approached Asnieres, I uttered a reflection that suddenly passed through my mind:

"To think that that bridge was cut in 1870! What was the good of it, pray, with Mont-Valerien just opposite?"

"It was idiotic," returned the decorated gentleman. "At that time I was on the staff of Admiral La Ronciere Le Noury. You have no conception, monsieur, of all the mistakes that were committed during the siege of Paris. Just fancy——"

Here the big man obligingly changed over into the corner seat, to be nearer me, leaving the pretty *brune* opposite the fair man; and he went on with his course in tactics, with broad gestures, pointing out to me the magnificent horizon, the Seine like a silver ribbon at the foot of the green slopes of Courbevoie, and, far in the background, Paris, with its houses and its monuments, among which stood out the gigantic silhouette of the Arc de Triomphe, dishonored by scaffoldings, and the gilded dome of the Invalides.

"Remember," continued the decorated gentleman, "that we were occupying the region near Clichy."

But I hardly heard him, for I saw with terror that, profiting by my maneuver, our two lovers had begun to whisper in smothered tones. The brief was still spread out on the young man's knees, for the looks of the thing, but it was easy to see that he no longer even cast a glance at it. And the train sped along, and the soldier, absorbed by his memories, went on with his discourse on military history that I feigned to listen to most devoutly, so as to draw his attention to the left side of the line.

We reach Saint-Cloud; we enter the tunnel, and in the pitch-darkness, on my word, I would swear that I heard the sound of a kiss. When we rush out again into the light, I cast a glance at the fair-haired man, who is once more deeply absorbed in his case. What do I make out on his left nostril but a funny little black spot. *Sapristi!* It is the patch, the killing patch, that in a thoughtless contact has loosened and passed from the lips of the dark beauty to the nose of her admirer.

I foresaw a horrible tragedy, for my tactician turned a questioning and suspicious look upon the lady, as if he had found something altered in her appearance, he hardly knew what. I would have given worlds to have been able to whisper to the good-looking young man: "For heaven's sake, remove that compromising patch at once, or you are betrayed!" Unfortunately, it was quite out of the question, seated as I was at a distance. So it seemed wiser to recall the officer's thoughts to the war of 1870, and the heights of Viroflay. But he no longer paid any heed to me. He chuckled in a sinister way behind his fierce mustache, gazing at the be-patched nose of the fair young man.

As for the woman, crimson, overcome with terror, she began to fan herself violently—a most distressing sight. What was going to happen? What terrible sentence was the implacable judge going to pronounce on the guilty wretches cowering beneath his gaze? Was I going to be obliged to look on, in this narrow railway carriage, at a challenge, a boxing-match, perhaps a butchery, a massacre?

Suddenly, to my intense relief, I caught sight of the three little yew-trees, trimmed into sugar-loaf shape, that guard the entrance into the Grand Monarch's town; a guard called out "Versailles! Versailles!" The train stopped. I got out, determined to stick to the officer to see what would happen. Judge of my stupor on seeing the lady take the fair man's arm and trip along at his side, while the decorated gentleman said to me, as he saw them disappear:

"They are charming. I know them. They live quite near me, in the Rue Duplessis. The husband is a lawyer. They are half-way through the honeymoon, as you might infer, sir. What a hug he gave her in the tunnel at Ville-d'Avray, to be sure!"

THE VIOLIN

WALKING the other day down the Rue de Provence, I stopped by chance at a curiosity shop, and raising my eyes found it was that of good Mme. Manchaballe, the mother of the little Manchaballes of the ballet. Manchaballe the second still needs filling out; but Manchaballe the first is superb. However, you must not imagine that that fact induced me to turn the handle of the door leading into the shop. No, I wanted to consult Mme. Manchaballe about the purchase of a bracelet, when my attention was drawn to a violin of antique aspect.

"Ah! Mme. Manchaballe, you sell musical instruments. Is that another string to your bow? or do you intend making Monsieur Pluque a present?"

"Not at all, M. Richard, not at all. I am not one of those mothers who try to influence the professors. I know what Judith is worth, and what Rebecca promises to be. I shall quietly await whatever fortune may have in store for my daughters. No, that violin is a good deed I tried to do."

I opened my eyes wide. I do not know why, but I could not imagine Mme. Manchaballe doing a good deed; I could not conceive her in such a position.

"Yes," she continued; "I sympathize with your surprise. And, after all, my act of charity was a failure, and I shan't try it again, I promise you. How much do you take the violin to be worth?"

I examined the instrument, which looked to me like a child's plaything, somewhat the worse for wear; and I replied without the least hesitation:

"I think it's worth—well a dozen francs, all told."

"Well, it cost me four hundred francs."

I jumped off my chair thinking it some amusing jest, but I noticed that behind her spectacles Mme. Manchaballe's eyes were wet with tears.

I am very soft-hearted, and if I see a crocodile weep, especially a lady crocodile, it touches me. I seized the old croco—I beg her pardon—Madame Manchaballe's hands, and said:

"Come, tell me all about it; you'll feel better then."

"Ah! M. Richard, you reopen the wound, but I can refuse you nothing. Well, one freezing morning Judith and Rebecca had swallowed their breakfast, and had started arm-in-arm for the eight o'clock class. I was dusting my china,—I'm the only woman who understands the art of dusting; it cannot be taught, it's a gift. l believe that my light hand accounts for the lightness of my daughter's legs,—when suddenly I see a little beggar girl, pretty, by Jove, very pretty even in her dirty rags. Ah! youth does not know its value! She enters, violin in hand, and asks alms. I refuse. It is one of my principles never to give to the poor I don't know, or even to those I do know. But the child began to sob:

"'Madame, have pity. It's to buy a bit of sausage for mamma, who is very hungry. At ten o'clock, when people are more awake, I sing in the streets, and then at noon I'll return the money. But, if you like, I can sing without accompaniment. So lend me twenty sous, and I'll leave you my violin in pledge, a very old violin that I had, from my great-grandfather, and which I wouldn't part with for the whole world; so you've nothing to fear.' Well, I didn't risk much. I kept the violin and lent the twenty sous."

"I beg your pardon, Mme. Manchaballe, you said four hundred francs——"

"Don't be impatient. About eleven o'clock a gentleman arrived who looked like some great diplomat. Oh! I can tell you he could not have made a better impression. He glances at my Renaissance Venus, my Louis Quinze clock, and suddenly stops at the violin. He takes it, feels it, listens to it, taps the case, and then says:

"'You've a real Stradivarius there!'

"'Impossible!'

"'It's so possible that I'll buy it of you for five hundred francs.'

"I felt quite giddy.

"'But the instrument isn't mine. It was only left here by an artist, who, it seems, will not part with it. He inherited it from his great-grandfather. However, he seemed very poor, and I lent him a few pence. In short; I've no doubt the matter can be arranged.'

"'Look here, Madame, get me the Stradivarius for five hundred francs, and there will be two hundred francs commission for you. It will cost me thirty-five louis; but bah, I can well afford such follies, and I'm sure to make· a good thing out of it.'

"'Very well, Monsieur,' I reply. 'Come back this afternoon; I'll speak to the artist.'

"And about noon my artist returns.

"I must be just; she brought me the twenty sous.

"'I am honest, Madame, and I thank you very much. Here is your money. Give me my violin!'

"'My dear,' I say, 'I've a proposal to make you that will overwhelm you with joy. I know an old gentleman who wants to buy your violin for three hundred francs.'"

"I beg pardon for interrupting, Madame Manchaballe, but you said five hundred francs."

"That is true, Monsieur; but you may make a mistake, even to your own advantage, and it seemed to me that fifteen louis was a very fair sum for the little good-for-nothing. I thought she would jump for joy. It was a fortune from the clouds for her, but she made a great fuss. She stuck to her instrument; it came to her from her great-grandfather; so that, to my deep regret, I had to go up to four hundred francs. I still had a little honorarium of five louis."

"Without reckoning the two hundred francs commission."

"Just so, not reckoning the commission. But business is business, and Rebecca and Judith cost me more than they earn—at least, just for the moment. At last my beggar makes up her mind, and as for reasons of my own, I did not wish her to meet the diplomat, I advanced the four hundred francs, and kept the Stradivarius."

"Well, Madame Manchaballe?"

"Well, Monsieur, it was all a plant. Good God! who is to be trusted if you can't put your confidence in people who look so highly respectable? The old gentleman was a notorious thief, and the little beggar girl was his accomplice, for I've not set eyes on either of them again, and I've the violin still on my hands."

THE PLEBE THAT TURNED

"WELL, the fun is beginning again at Saint-Cyr," said the Colonel, looking up from his newspaper.

"The war between the seniors and the 'melons' has broken out afresh."

"A great thing, this hazing," observed Captain Brulard, as he stirred his absinthe scientifically. "We couldn't break in the young colts without it."

"It depends on the character of the colt, I think. There are some sensitive natures that knocks and pin-pricks don't suit."

"Sensitive natures? Yours, for instance?"

"Yes, mine," said the Colonel. "My military career came very near terminating in a tragedy."

"Let's have the story, Colonel."

"Well, I must tell you, in the first place, that when I entered the imperial military school of Saint-Cyr I did not come from a course at a *lycée* where I had been in the habit of giving and receiving blows without attaching any particular importance to them. I had been brought up at home with the respect due to my position, and was already a gentleman, and a proud one, ready to exact from others the same polite consideration that I always extended, to them. The good *abbé*, my tutor, was a little anxious about my haughty disposition. He tried to instill in me a proper respect for seniors, and he taught me the famous 'Prayer of the Melons,' which dates, I believe, from 1807.

> "'Senior adored,
>   Angel of light,
> By "melons" implored
>   From morning till night.
> When we rise with the dawn

Thy name we all bless;
May thy glorious shadow
Never grow less!'

"For the first week everything went well. The upper classmen had not yet arrived, and we plebes were masters of the field.

"We wandered at our own sweet will over the grounds, subject only to the supervision of some old *sergents-d'ours*, or 'cub breakers,' who taught us to stow our effects neatly in our chests, to varnish our boots, pipe-clay our belts and make our beds.

"As the nights were cool and the courts dark, we used to pass the evenings in two large rooms, consecrated to such reunions.

"The rooms were unfurnished and cheerless, but they were warm and well lighted.

"One was known, in the slang of the school, as *le Turc*, the other as *l'Anglais*.

"Here we solaced ourselves with impromptu and irregular concerts. We were yet in blissful ignorance of the fact that *le Turc*, which was larger and better ventilated than *l'Anglais*, had been appropriated by the seniors for their own exclusive use.

"At last the seniors arrived.

"We were arranged in two ranks along the wall, the great doors were flung open and the seniors marched in, preceded by a drum-major and a band.

"How fine they looked, with their mustaches and side-whiskers, their smart uniforms and kepis! We cut a sorry figure beside them, with our fatigue dress and unmilitary carriage.

"They drew up in battle array opposite us. This evolution puzzled me, but not for long, for the whole three hundred of them suddenly charged us, smote us hip and thigh, and drove us, with blows and kicks, to an open shed which was used for drills on rainy days.

"My comrades whispered to me that this was only a time-honored usage, but I was furious, nevertheless. I was therefore foolish enough to offer some slight resistance, whereupon a dozen seniors fell upon me at once, crying:

"'So you resist, do you, *Monsieur Bazar?*'

"It was a bad beginning, and I immediately became noted as an obstinate malcontent.

"That evening, while we were at dinner, General Gondrecourt, the commandant of the school, came into the mess-hall.

"Each of us received a glass of champagne. The General raised his glass and said:

"'Gentlemen, the manner in which the recruits have just been welcomed by the seniors by no means meets with my approval. This barbarous and brutal custom is not in accord with modern civilization. I therefore propose that we drink a glass to the abolition of hazing.'

"A dead silence followed this conciliatory speech, and I observed, with consternation, that not one of the seniors drank to the toast.

"'Well, gentlemen, silence gives consent,' the General resumed, ignoring the seniors' abstinence. 'We will consider hazing abolished.'

"But now there were murmurs from all parts of the hall, together with the crowing of cocks and the smashing of plates.

"The General, not wishing to compromise the dignity of his shoulder-straps by remaining among the turbulent cadets, quickly withdrew from the scene. Poor Gondrecourt! He was a visionary, like Trochu and many another French general. He had great confidence in the power of words, and forgot that a soldier's duty is to act, not to talk.

"After dinner I lighted a cigarette and repaired to *le Turc*, in expectation of the usual amateur concert.

"But alas! on entering I ran against a senior corporal, to that gentleman's profound surprise and indignation.

"'*Un melon au Turc!*' he sang out, and two of his classmates ran up, also yelling: '*Un melon au Turc!*'

"I began to have an inkling of the enormity of my crime. I teamed afterwards that so flagrant a case of high treason had never occurred before.

"'Monsieur—' I began, very politely.

"'Call me Corporal, Corporal Julian.'

"'Corporal, I was not aware that the *Turc* was a place of amusement forbidden to the first-year men.'

"'Ah! You argue, do you, melon? Sour melon! Green melon! Dirty melon! Rotten melon! Monsieur Bazar turns rusty, eh? Well, since you think the *Turc* is a place of amusement, we will amuse you!'

"Thereupon three of them seized me, and, despite my struggles, stood me on my bead in a tub of water until I was nearly drowned. When they set me on my feet again I walked up to Julian, beside myself with rage.

"'Corporal Julian,' I said, 'my name is Raoul de Giverny. I am only a "melon" now, but in two years I shall be an officer. Then—I shall kill you!'

"Indeed, the affair might have been settled then and there, but we were separated, and I was put under arrest for having insulted a superior.

"From that time forth my life was a martyrdom.

"Julian had passed the word to his comrades and I was subjected to what they called the Prussian system. Punishments fell on my head like hailstones. Whenever I met Julian he would say, with a sneer:

"'Ah! We'll tame that savage disposition of yours, Monsieur Bazar! We'll tame it, never fear!'

"'Perhaps,' I answered, on more than one occasion, ' but I shall kill you all the same.'

"To kill him—that became my fixed idea. I counted the months, the days that must elapse before the blessed moment would arrive when I, as an officer, would be privileged to take my revenge. But I had one great anxiety. I feared that the long list of my reprimands, punishments and orders of arrest might compel me to remain a 'melon' for a second year.

"In the midst of these personal worries came, like a thunderclap, the news that war was declared against Prussia.

"On the fourteenth of July all the seniors were commissioned sub-lieutenants, by imperial order. They left the school on the same day. Julian, who had been assigned to the Forty-second Regiment of the line, was wild with joy.

"He called out to me as he was leaving:

"'Au revoir, Monsieur Bazar. I bear you no malice. Try to become sensible, won't you?'

"All of which soothed my feelings immensely!

"Events took place rapidly in those days. Three weeks later we, the 'melons,' also became sub-lieutenants. No account was taken of arrests or bad records. I was assigned to the Fourth Dragoons, and hastened to join my regiment, which was encamped at Metz, before the Mazelle gate.

"We were in action at Borny, at Gravelotte and at St. Privat. The constant excitement of those days, I must admit, almost made me forget Corporal Julian and my plans of vengeance.

"They were recalled to me suddenly on the thirty-first of August, the day of the famous sortie, when I saw an infantry regiment marching out, company front, and on one of the flanks Julian, still wearing the blue-striped trousers of Saint-Cyr, with the gold stripe of his rank hastily sewed on the sleeves of his school tunic.

"He recognized me, hesitated a moment, then came toward me and said:

"'Monsieur Bazar, we are marching against the enemy. Perhaps I have been a little hard on you. I do not know when I shall be able to give you satisfaction. Meanwhile, I want to beg your pardon. Tell me, won't you, that you have no hard feelings?'

"He held out his hand so frankly, so cordially, that, my faith! I was carried away by emotion. I leaned from my saddle, threw my arms around my enemy's neck, and we embraced like two brothers.

"'Au revoir!' he called back, as he hurried off to rejoin his company.

"Almost at the same instant the firing began, and amid the thunder of artillery we received orders to advance to the relief of the hotly engaged infantry.

"Suddenly, at a turning of the road, among a confused mass of corpses, I saw poor Julian, dead and stiff in his Saint-Cyr tunic, with a hole in his forehead.

"Impulsively and instinctively I saluted with my drawn saber as I dashed past, and it seemed to me that he smiled, as if glad that I had forgiven the rude jests that had made me so earnestly long for his death—his death that now brought tears to my eyes! And I fervently repeated the Prayer of the Melons:

> "'When we rise with the dawn
>   Thy name we all bless;
> May thy glorious shadow
>   Never grow less.'"

THE REHEARSAL

"WELL, what luck?" I asked Mme. Bourrimel, my concierge, as I came in the other evening. Her daughter Leona, you must know, had presented herself for examination at the Conservatoire that day, and I always make a point of appearing interested in my concierge's family affairs. I find it pays to do so.

"Ah, M. Richard, you come at just the right moment. I was longing for somebody to talk to about it. Sit down there in my armchair by the latchstring, and I will tell you the whole story.

"Well, as you know, Leona had learned the role of Blanche in *Le Roi s'amuse*.

"My husband—you know his political opinions—chose the piece. He thought it would be a good thing to show the people the goings of the kings in the old days before we had this blessed republic. Besides, it is by Victor Hugo, you know, and it seems to be fairly well written. Leona's teacher—that fat little M. Guillemot with the red cheeks, you know, and a very nice man he is, too, I must say and always very polite to me—well, the teacher made no objection, and so Leona studied up the part of Blanche.

"'She seems to have been created expressly for the role,' M. Guillemot often said to me. 'She is Blanche herself.'

"She selected for the examination the scene in the second act in which Blanche confesses to Dame Berarde her love for the king. We went through it several times at home after supper.

"The prince, ever kind and attentive, held the book, and I took the part of Dame Berarde, which was quite suited to my years. There's a ring at the bell, M. Richard. Please pull the cord. Thanks. Where was I? Oh, yes; I remember.

"Leona knew her lines so well that she could have spoken them backward.

"The prince had ordered her costume and had even been good enough to go with her when she went to try it on.

"'You need not leave your post, Mme. Bourrimel,' he said. 'I will attend to everything.'

"Ah, but that costume was superb! Imagine a foulard with honeysuckles and humming birds on a white ground, the skirt trimmed with three bands of purple velvet, square cut bodice, point lace sleeves—but I forget. You are a man, and you can't imagine it.

"But when I saw that dress my maternal heart leaped for joy, and I threw my arms around the prince's neck and exclaimed, 'With such a dress as that Leona cannot help making a success, and it will be all owing to your generosity.'

"Indeed, M. Richard, I was deeply moved, I assure you, and the prince himself was much affected. I thought I saw tears behind his glasses. Well, the great day came at last, and we all set out for the Conservatoire, accompanied by our neighbor, Mme. Frimard, and her daughter, who has tried the examination in comedy for the last six years and failed every time.

"But, M. Richard, the bell has rung three times. Please open."

"I beg pardon, Mme. Bourrimel, I am a green concierge, remember."

"Where was I? Oh, to be sure, at the Conservatoire. Leona went to the stage door with Mlle. Frimard, who was to take the part of Dame Berarde, and Mme. Frimard and I got seats together in the little red theater. They call it 'Etruscan,' I believe, but it is quite pretty for all that.

"Of course the prince, being connected with the Russian embassy, could not be with us. He sat in a proscenium box, right behind the president's wife. Ah, there's a lady who knows how to dress! I couldn't keep my eyes off the bright yellow capote perched on top of her shiny black hair.

"Of course Mme. Frimard, whose daughter had been going through the mill so long, knew all the critics and the members of the jury, and she pointed them out to me while we were waiting for Leona to appear.

"That fat man, sound asleep, was Maurice Tourcey. He always slept at these exhibitions.

"The dark, shabby man was Victor Fessard, who had left politics for literature at the age of 50 and now slashed right and left to make people think he knew all about it, just as people hiss bullfights to pretend they are Spaniards.

"The gentleman with the long hair and the big mustache was La Puiseraye, who was kindness itself, and the man who looked like a general was Auguste Destu, an honest man and a scholar.

"Then, in the jury box, there was Dumas, the smiling Jules Claretie, the amiable Halevy. The shriveled-looking person was Camille Doucet.

"The old man in the middle, with a head like a grand priest's, was the president, Ambroise Thomas, and the merry, mocking silhouette in the last row was Cadet, of the Comedie Francaise. It was great fun for me. Mme. Frimard knew them all very well, she had been to see them so often on her daughter's account.

"Now and then the prince leaned forward from his seat in the official box and gave me a little confidential smile with a sort of wink, which meant, 'I cannot be with you in person on account of my official position, but I am with you in spirit.'

"Wasn't it nice of him?

"At last, after several other debutantes had appeared, Leona's turn came. There was a moment of silence, and the master of ceremonies announced:

"Mlle. Leona Bourrimel, aged 20 years, appeared last year and the year before without success'—Why did the wretch have to say that?—'assumes the role of Blanche in *Le Roi s'amuse*, assisted by Mlle. Frimard.'

"Ah, M. Richard, you don't know how I felt! You are not a mother. My heart was in my—Oh, the second floor is waiting for his candle! Please hand it to him through the window. Thanks.

"About Leona's scene. I must say that the management was very mean about the stage setting. A table with a green cloth, two plush chairs—that was all. What would they say if we should come to their theater in rags, I should like to know?

"But, ah, how pretty Leona looked when she came on, with her flowered gown and her old fashioned cape with steel clasps. A murmur of admiration ran through the theater. M. Dumas twirled his mustache, and M. Halevy adjusted his opera glass—both good signs. As for M. Tourcey, he kept on sleeping, but it seems that this never interferes with his ability to criticize—not in the least. When Leona, as Blanche, confessed her love for the king, she looked at straight at Prince Tapaloff.

"Ah, M. Richard, if you had seen and heard her! She was the living, loving Blanche, and one could feel the force of the passion that consumed her. The jury felt it evidently, for they became intensely absorbed and excited, the little dried up man especially. And at his age!

"My daughter went on with her lines, which described the noble appearance of the king, his graceful bearing in the saddle and so forth, and still she kept her eyes fixed on the prince. She surely could do no less after what he had done for her—the gown, the cape, the jewels and all the rest.

"Of course the lines referred to King Francis I, but the prince no doubt saw in them a delicate allusion to himself, and he smiled in a way that showed he was much gratified. And indeed he, too, is a tall, handsome gentleman and a splendid horseman. One might have fancied that Victor Hugo had him in mind when he wrote the lines.

"The president's wife smiled also. Perhaps she was thinking of the present ruler of France. But all of a sudden some crank cried, 'Face the audience!'

"The cry was taken up and repeated frow all parts of the room. 'Yes; face the audience! Never mind the fine people in the boxes!'

"The fools! Just imagine, they thought that Leona was looking at and playing at the president's wife, and so they were jealous!

"I rose in my place and said in a loud voice, but with great dignity:

"'But she is not looking at Mme. la Presidente. She does not care that (I snapped my fingers) for Mme. la Presidente. She is looking at Prince Tapaloff.'

"At this the disturbance increased. In the midst of laughter, yells and hisses I turned to the jury and added:

"'I should think I ought to know. I am her mother.'

"Then there was a fearful row, Leona could not go on, the jury retired and presently, by M. Thomas' orders, I was thrust out of doors in company with Mme. Frimard, who, as her daughter's lines had been thus cut off, protested as angrily as I did.

"And that's the way that Leona, through a silly mistake of the audience, has again failed to get the *prix*. For my part, as soon as I saw the prince, I said, with great dignity:

"'My daughter's career is ruined and through you. If you have the instincts of a gentleman, you will know your duty and perform it.'

"The prince's conduct, I must admit was perfect.

"'Mme. Bourrimel,' he said, 'I am a gentleman, and I know my duty, which will also be my pleasure. I will marry Leona at once. We will leave for Dieppe tonight, and you and your husband shall join us within a month.'

"And, in fact, he did marry her, and they went off on the 8 o'clock express. Ah, M. Richard, I begin to think there is a future in store for us."

"All's well that ends well," I said.

"Allow me to return you your armchair and latchstring. Good evening, Mme. Bourrimel."

MR. JEFFERSON'S ADVERTISEMENT

ENTERING his magnificent mansion on Michigan Avenue, in which all the modern improvements, such as electric lights, telephones and elevators, could be found, Mr. Samuel Jefferson seated himself in a leather-covered armchair, mounted his feet on the mantelpiece, and became absorbed in melancholy reflection. He was evidently rich, very rich. His trade in Wyoming in salt pork had been a prodigious success, and he had in his employ at least one hundred farmers and as many cowboys.

But all his vast wealth had come to him late in life. His youth had been passed in a veritable struggle for existence. His poor wife, Jenny, had died of misery long ago, leaving to his care a dozen children, whom he had brought up as best he could. The boys had found employment and married, but the girls, Annie, Deborah and Margaret, in default of a sufficient *dot*, had remained old maids. This had not robbed them of their good looks, but it had soured their tempers.

Fortune came, however, at last, and the Misses Jefferson had now the finest equipages of New York, electric coupés and steam victorias. Their gowns were made at Poncet's, in Paris, and their hats at Birot's, while at their service were no end of needlewomen and tiring maids, veritable slaves, white or black, ready to carry out all their wishes. Interminable discussions arose continually in the handsome home on Michigan Avenue, and the life of the poor *pater familias* was by no means full of happiness.

"Who will relieve me of my girls?" he groaned, as he puffed great clouds of smoke from an enormous cigar.

Mechanically he took the New York *Herald* and reread on the third page, an advertisement he had inserted, which ran as follows:

> A father of a family, desirous of marrying his daughters, offers a pretty choice and a handsome marriage portion to an honorable young man who may be willing to choose one of the ladies for his wife, and who will lead her to the altar at the Parish Church, on 326th Avenue, the marriage to be there celebrated by the Reverend Brother Bright. The fortune promised has been made honorably in a business eminently national in character. Apply directly to Number 724 Michigan Avenue, where all particulars will be given.
>
> N. B.—The young girls may be interviewed from two to five o'clock P. M. daily, Sundays and holidays excepted, no one being received after four o'clock.

Eight days had passed, eight anxious days, since the insertion of the advertisement had been decided upon as a last resource. He had said nothing to his daughters respecting the means he had adopted for securing their marriage, the shame of the publicity of which was heightened by the fact that no suitor had yet appeared. Was he to have eternally the care of Annie, Deborah and Margaret, who were growing older and older daily, and more and more quarrelsome and bad tempered?

While he was reflecting upon the subject, a servant entered with a card, on which Jefferson read the words:

SAMUEL SPRING,
Solicitor.

"A lawyer! Show him in." The servant ushered in a little blond man, with a pointed beard and a decided manner. He bowed with an almost imperceptible movement of the head, and seated himself in the arm-chair, indicated by his host. After having lighted a cigar, he said:

"Sir, I read an advertisement in the New York *Herald* which you inserted relative to your daughters. My card has told you my name, and also indicated my profession. I make, good or bad, yearly, from twenty to thirty thousand dollars; I have never had a cold in my head, and no one in my family has as yet been hanged. I consider myself an absolutely honorable person."

Jefferson replied with a joy not assumed:

"Sir, believe me, I am greatly flattered by your choice."

"Now," continued Spring, "will you not permit me to ask you a few questions, not only respecting the physical and moral qualities of your daughters, but also regarding their personal estate—the total amount. Business, you know, is business, and and I do not hesitate to say that on this point I found your advertisement a little vague."

"I am ready to furnish all the necessary information."

"All right!" replied Spring. "Commence, if you wish, with Miss Margaret; she is the youngest, I believe."

"Yes, sir. Margaret is about twenty-six years of age; she is as beautiful as the flowers in spring. She has sunlight in her golden hair, every charm in her blue eyes, and all the perfume in——"

"Come, come, no poetry; be exact. What does she weigh?"

"Dressed, she weighs 122 pounds."

"Her height?"

"Four feet, five inches, excellent digestion, fine voice. She sings admirably our national air, Yankee Doodle."

"That will do. And now the marriage portion?"

"I will give her fifty thousand dollars."

The lawyer made a grimace.

"That's not much."

"But," continued the father, "you should remember, twenty-six years, golden hair, blue eyes, and spring——"

"Ta-ta! Tell me now of number two."

"My number two," continued Jefferson, slightly disconcerted, "is Deborah. If Margaret is the spring blossom, Deborah is the summer flower in full bloom. Her eyes are fringed with long lashes, her hair luxuriant and black, and her chest is well developed. She is just five feet, and an adorable woman. She weighs one hundred and thirty pounds, and has an appetite like an ogre. She has no particular talent. There are those who prefer a woman of that type."

"You have not told me her age."

"I have told you that she is in the very summer of life. She is thirty-five years old, and I will give her one hundred thousand dollars as a marriage portion."

"That's better, but still a small sum. How about number three?"

"Ah, my number three is Annie, and she, above all others, will make an exquisite wife. With her it is the autumn of life, with all its melancholy, all its discretion, its tenderness. She is five feet, two inches tall, her arms and shoulders are wonderfully beautiful. She has a decided talent for housekeeping and can make you the finest gin cocktail that can be brewed for a night-cap."

"What is her age? Do not be afraid; speak frankly."

"I will hide nothing from you. She has just passed her fortieth year. She is not exactly a young girl, but I increase the marriage portion *pro rata*. I give with her one hundred and fifty thousand dollars."

"You said forty years and one hundred and fifty thousand?"

"I did, and I should say it is a tidy sum."

Samuel Spring reflected a moment while puffing great clouds of tobacco smoke, that curled above his head in blue spiral waves. Suddenly he seemed to have an inspiration.

"Tell me, sir," he said, "—it is more than possible that we will come to an understanding regarding your daughters—but have you, by any chance, among the lot, one of about fifty years of age, and would the same *pro rata* be observed?"

A BEAR AND A BRIGADIER

THE BRIGADIER DES ESBROUFFTEES threw a melancholy glance at the door of the guard-room which the Marshal of the guardhouse was noisily closing, then, after a moment of reflection, he sat down on the sunken camp-bed whose boards were to take the place of his elastic hair-mattress, drew from his pocket a pencil and some paper and wrote upon his knees:

Aug. 17, 18—. My Dear Mother:—I shall not be able to open the hunting season at La Chataigne-raye this year! The Thirty-fifth Hussars will make no maneuvers, and I was glad to think I could pass a happy week at the chateau, as of old, when I was a collegian and had vacations. But I am held for thirty days in the guard-room. Ah! "Thirty days in the guard-room!" You will believe that I have set fire to the quarters, deserted to the enemy, or sold my country. For a civilian to be sentenced to a month in prison he must have committed a serious misdeed. In our profession it has been sufficient to have bought a bear. "But," you say, "why in the name of heaven, unlucky boy, did you buy a bear?" Ah! my good mother, let us see, hand upon conscience, have you never bought things which were absolutely useless to you, for nothing, for vain glory? I have hitherto been too busy with maneuvers, classes, theories, tasks, for frolics. But a fair has just been held near our quarters. A mountebank there made two bears, one brown and one black, dance to the sound of a hurdy-gurdy. The black one was especially delightful. While dancing he struck attitudes, made queer faces, and swung himself about in a way to make one die of laughter.

At any rate, I said to the mountebank, "Monsieur, is it difficult to make the bear dance?"

"Oh! not at all," the man answered. "You have only to take the string, like that, in the left hand, and with the right hand over the left arm hit the animal little blows with this stick. You must look at him all the time and keep yourself at a distance. Try it first."

I tried it, rather awkwardly. Bless me! I was not used to it—a maneuver not taught cadets. I took the string; I crossed my right arm over my left arm; I patted the creature with the stick, and, O joy! O intoxicating fun! the black beast began to dance. I was enchanted

"How much is your black bear worth?" I asked then, in a burst of enthusiasm.

"Five hundred francs."

It was a little dear, but I thought only of the amusement I should have with my comrades. I could pose as the tamer, and pretend that it was a bear I myself had brought from the Pyrenees. I haggled over it and succeeded in getting the animal for four hundred and fifty francs. It appeared that it was given to me all the more that

I had the small stick and the string over the bargain. I paid the money, to the stupefaction of the people, astonished to see so much gold in the purse of a simple Brigadier of Hussars, and was going away with my love of a black bear. But at first he did not want to follow me; he regretted his master, poor thing! And then, who knows? perhaps he had a friendship for the brown bear. I pulled the string, I moved my stick over my left arm without taking my eyes off of my companion! This obliged me to walk with my head turned and without seeing where I was going. One does not imagine how difficult it may be to perform things which appear the most simple.

At last my bear rose—he was almost as large as I am—and, amid general merriment, behold us going toward the cavalry quarters. All along the way I heard jests, calls, peals of laughter, which I thought led to success.

Together we entered the gate of the quarters under the eyes of the dumbfounded sentinel. It was just at the hour for grooming the horses, they were all attached to the wall by forage-ropes passed through the rings. The men with gray caps on their heads and with bare arms had placed the buckets behind them on a line formed by the sponges and cloths, and had their currycombs ready to begin the toilette of the horses. The marshals were making their ten steps before their platoons, and, in the center, the captain of the week with the officers of service received the roll-call from marshals of headquarters. Everybody was on deck. I had arrived at a good time.

I entered bravely, leading my lively and comical companion and flourishing my stick. And all at once—ah! my good mother, a thunderbolt falling in the middle of the court could not have produced more effect, nor more of a hubbub. Imagine six hundred horses breaking away, kicking over the pails and buckets, bounding around me, distracted, neighing with terror, while the men yelled, the officers swore and the stablemen ran in every direction with snaffle bridles in their hands.

It appears that horses have a mad fear of bears. One is instructed every day, but I was absolutely ignorant of that detail of natural history.

During this time ten of the horses had rushed out and away across the streets, running over people and breaking down fences.

"At least shut the gates!" thundered the captain of the week. This order was executed in haste, while in the midst of the general tumult my black bear kept on dancing. Then the captain addressed me.

"Here! Brigadier des Esbroufftees, are you crazy or drunk? Do you think you can bring your foolery here to throw the whole troop into disorder? Go to the guard-room. I shall report you to the Colonel. As to your bear, arrange to have him taken away at once."

I called Perdriol, my orderly, and said to him: "Listen, I paid four hundred and fifty francs for that animal, string included, to a mountebank exhibiting at the fair. Tell him that now I will give him another one hundred francs if he will take the creature back and relieve me of him."

"But Brigadier, I never led a bear!"

I showed him the system of little blows of the stick over the left arm, and while he went off with the beast who was always frisking—it was, indeed, the moment to dance!— I followed the Marshal of the guard-house, who bore me away jingling his bunch of keys and making malicious jokes.

Presently I saw Perdriol coming back.

"Brigadier, the mountebank had gone and I have not been able to find him."

"What did you do then?"

"I brought back your bear; his return produced more of an uproar than ever, and the captain, exasperated, has ordered him to be shot. See, now!"

I went to the window and I saw my poor animal being led to the shooting-target. He went along in torture, always dancing. He was a brave fellow, and, I know not why, there came to me a vague remembrance of the Duke d'Inghien and of the dungeon of Vincennes.

My bear was placed erect before a line of men; he continued to balance gracefully, having doubtless refused to have his eyes bandaged. A detonation resounded; he fell, struck by six balls directed to his heart—and one knows that our hussars aim well.

With tears in my eyes, I looked on his execution for which, with due regard for proportion, I am as responsible as Napoleon III. for that of the Emperor Maximilian. As to myself, I told you in the beginning, I have thirty days in the guard-room—"For introducing in the quarters a ferocious beast that turned everything topsy-turvy, caused the breakage of two hundred fetters, a hundred and fifty bridoons, forty pails, twenty buckets, the wounding of two guards, and the gravest accidents in the streets."

This is why, my dear mother, I cannot come home to open the hunting season. Decidedly, we live in very strange times and it becomes more and more difficult to amuse ourselves a bit.

Your poor unhappy brigadier,
PHILIP.

THAT CHURCH PICTURE

TO M. RAOUL DE PARABÈRE, Captain Twentieth Cuirassiers,

      Paris, France:

My dear boy and ex-pupil—You remember, I am very sure, the numerous punishments I was forced to inflict upon you in your youthful days for your too pronounced taste for sketching, and sketching upon any and all things. Even my prayer-books were covered with outlines, not always as correct as they should have been, that came from your pen. I also know that at St. Cyr this talent of yours had not its equal. Briefly, with these facts in mind, you are the man I want. But now to explain this preamble.

Since your school-days I have become the curé of Avricourt, a small parish by no means rich and with a church decidedly shabby, weather-worn, and with one of the panels of the wall in a condition that truly afflicts me. It has a spot upon it produced by moisture—in fact, a former leak—some three meters long by as many high, and which I desire to conceal by a picture of the same dimensions. It has occurred to me that perhaps you could find this prize for me in Paris, at auction possibly or in some kindred establishment. But I must limit you as to price, since the committee who have the settlement for the picture in charge will pay for same but five and fifty francs, frame included. Only select a Biblical subject, from the Old or New Testament as suits you—for the rest I rely entirely upon you. Attend to this immediately, and may heaven keep you, my own dear lad. Your old and affectionate preceptor,

MIGUEL, Curé of Avricourt.

To M. L'abbé Miguel, Curé of Avricourt,
    Province of A——, France:

My Dear Abbé—I will start the campaign at once, though a picture three meters square or thereabouts, at five and fifty francs, frame included, is not a very easy thing to find. However, I shall do my best; count upon me.

Your old and grateful pupil,
    Parabère, Captain Twentieth Cuirassiers.

When Raoul de Parabère had written and sent off this short and somewhat laconic letter—he was a busy man with his garrison duties and had a limited number of hours in the day to devote to his own amusement—he sat himself down and began to reflect with seriousness upon the task before him.

"Simply a gigantic task!" he told himself. How the deuce was he to find a Biblical picture of these huge dimensions, and how the deuce could he possibly spare a moment to hunt for it? He saw himself demanding from the commandant a leave of absence upon such a commission! He'd certainly send him to the right-about and to the devil besides!

But Raoul de Parabère, with all his faults, had an excellent heart. So the more he thought of the little church and its needs, the more he felt inclined to make the attempt; and as the curé, of whom he was really very fond, had written him to be in haste about it, he might as well start at once on his first essay.

And Parabère, leaping to his feet, dismissed his orderly and his waiting mount, hailed a passing *fiacre* and ran to the Hôtel de Ventes, the likeliest place he could think of at the moment and where he found everything but what he sought—a Biblical picture. And the next day, and the day after and the day after that, between the hours of official duty and a few other things, Parabére followed precisely the same trail—in addition rummaged the bric-à-brac shops and the stalls for odds and ends—still without success.

He had really begun to despair, when he recalled the shop of a certain Mme. Lardêche, an old acquaintance of his, who knew where to put her finger, day or night, upon those charming trifles in Sèvres and those trinkets so necessary to bestow upon friends who of course love you for yourself alone.

In this marvellous collection of Mme. Lardêche's one always had a choice of pretty things that had an air of costing nothing at all till you came to pay for them—and then!

But what did that matter when every article in the establishment had a number, history, and genealogical tree to prove its antiquity?

"I shall certainly not find at her house, my picture or any other picture at five-and-fifty francs, frame included, thought Parabère, disconsolately, "still it's the last chance, and if the price runs above the mark, *parbleu!* I'll make up the figure."

And he entered to find Mme. Lardêche, as usual, like a gorgeous spider awaiting her prey, enthroned in a Mme. de Maintenon chair, and, truly, not unlike that lady herself, with her touch of rouge upon the cheekbones, her patches, and her lust of gold.

"Ah, is it you, my captain?" she exclaimed on seeing him enter, "is it really you? and a whole month since you paid me a call! You've changed your mind, then, and decided to take that bit of Sèvres for Mlle. Regnier of the Gaîté? A lovely trifle!"

"No, my dear Mme. Lardêche, my errand today is a serious one. I am seeking a picture, a church picture—think of it!—some three to five meters square," and as Parabère talked on, unfolding to her the mission he was expected to fill, the face of Mme. Lardêche expanded, more and more, into a broad and unctuous smile.

"A providence!" she cried. "A providence in truth! I have precisely what you want, above there," pointing to the loft—"a church picture and by a great painter; but so huge, so very huge, that no one would ever buy it. I will sell it to you, M. de Parabère, for the merest song."

"Bravo! and this church picture represents"

"I do not know, that is, exactly; something taken from sacred history; still, if you want a special subject—"

"No, no, not at all," said Parabère, alarmed lest the prize should slip through his fingers; "the subject is a matter of positive indifference to me, provided it is Biblical and the canvas of the requisite size."

"Three to five meters, you said? Oh, it's all of that! But, come, see it for yourself; it's here in the loft."

"The loft? No, thanks, I'm pressed for time as it is. I leave it to your judgment. What do you want for it?"

"Frame included? *Eh, bien*, fifty louis—dirt cheap at that."

"I'll give you thirty; boxing and expressage prepaid. Address the Abbé Miguel, Curé of Avricourt, to be shipped immediately. Do you agree?"

Mme. Lardêche battled a moment. The picture was immense! the painting superb! the frame a veritable antique. Then—she yielded and the bargain was sealed.

Two hours later the worthy Curé Miguel, at his frugal tea, received a message destined to set the parish wild with delight:

Picture purchased, superb, right size, five and fifty francs, frame included, boxed, expressed, and shipped. PARABÈRE.

It was but little after daylight the next morning when the Curé Miguel gathered together the committees on funds and arrangements, and laid before them not only the good news of the picture's coming, but also, with a certain prideful pomp, the necessity for its proper reception. He could scarcely believe that that spot of humidity, which had so long distracted and divided his attention with his religious duties, was going to disappear at last, to actually pass from sight behind the radiant colors of a broad and glowing canvas—all for the insignificant sum of five and fifty francs!

To skip details, however, and, the discussion that followed between the abbé and the committees—torn between a desire to greet the picture with all due honor and the natural economy of all church committees—it was finally decided that nothing short of a grand procession could fill the bill and still please all parties.

The abbé himself, as curé of the church, attended by his acolytes, the choir and chorister boys, was to lead the cortége and escort the box to the sacristy of the chapel, where it was to be opened in the presence of the assembled people; and Mme. la Duchesse de Precy-Brussac, the head of the reception committee, was to set to work immediately upon the fashioning of gorgeous garlands and the erection of a suitable and imposing *reposoir.*

A *reposoir* constructed from the park benches arranged in a square, decorated with colored streamers, all the available casts of holy saints to be borrowed in the neighborhood, a number of china vases, and a limitless quantity of trailing vines and potted flowers.

But, with all these preparations, it was fully twelve o'clock before the procession, which had swelled to a big one, was well under way, the participants walking two by two; the cure and the Little Sisters of the Poor, at the head of the line, under a beautiful banner of purple satin embroidered with gold. Next came the choir and the chorister boys, followed by the van from the police station, hung with white and wreathed with blossoms, thanks again to the taste of Mme. la Duchesse.

Flanking this chariot, and presenting a most martial aspect with their brass helmets sparkling and shining in the rays of the sun, marched the brave Captain Balligan and his corps of firemen. Behind the firemen came the beadle of the church, behind the beadle the greater part of the population of the village of Avricourt, among whom one saw, resplendent, the Duke and Duchess of Precy-Brussac, the distributor of contributions, and the lieutenant of gendarmerie. Only the Maire, his assistant and the schoolmaster, for the sake of example, had consented to stay at home.

And all along the route the choir sang psalms and praises, the choristers swung their censers; the station-master came a square to meet them to tell them the box had already arrived; and, when the curé had blessed it and four of the firemen had lifted and shouldered it to its place in the wagon, the long procession faced about and returned majestically across the plain.

The incense mingled its intoxicating breath with the resinous odor of woods and fields, the voices of the singers rose and fell in soft and rhythmic cadence, repeated by the voice of the distant hills, and everywhere throughout the country the peasants, men and women, abandoned their work to stand with gaping mouths and uncovered heads as the great box passed on its way.

The curé had only one regret, that his dear lad, Raoul de Parabère, was absent and could not witness the crowning triumph of his efforts. But words fail me. Picture for yourself that fateful moment when, at last, the box was placed in the sacristy and the carpenter, old Père Virgile, on his knees beside it, made the nails leap from the planks that had shielded it on the way; while at his elbow, on her knees too, was the directress of the Little Sisters of the Poor, whom the worthy curé had selected from all that multitude for the final lifting of the veil. Picture for yourselves, also, the amazement of the faithful, when the good Sœur Anne, folding back with eager fingers the baize that still curtained the face of the picture, dropped it again instantly, as if it burned her, and with a cry that certainly sounded like a cry of horror.

"Well, well, my sister," cried the curé, impatiently, believing her, in his innocent soul, only bewildered by the beauty of the picture, "off with it, please; off with it."

"Off with it? Pardon me, M. le Curé," and Sœur Anne rose up crimson as a poppy, "there is some mistake; I do not wish to unveil this picture!"

"You do not wish it?" repeated the curé, bewildered in his turn, "you do not wish to unveil the picture? So be it, Sœur Anne, so be it! Captain Balligan, will you oblige us?"

And the captain would and did—that is, to the extent of one corner; but though he gazed longer and with more admiration than the directress had done, the picture's face was not unveiled when the gallant fireman stumbled to his feet.

"I—I am not a judge," said he, with a defensive air and an added redness upon his florid cheeks, "and if you please, M. le Curé——"

The captain got no farther in his little speech; the Duc de Precy-Brussac, out of patience with so much humming, hawing, and delay, had stepped behind him, and in the twinkling of an eye the picture was seen by all. By all!

And what is more, it was seen by the men with "ohs" and "ahs"; by the women with cries and blushes; by the good Sœur Anne with a frantic bound and an active wheeling of her youthful charges' faces to the wall.

"Bread and water and a week of penance to every one," she cried, "who dares to look around!"

The trouble?

The picture, of course! The picture of a nobly fashioned dame, reclining upon a couch, her costume, that of an undraped artist's model, who retains by the hem of his garment (a coat of many colors) the equally noble figure of a struggling man, seeking with might and main to run away—an artist's rendering of a

Biblical story, Joseph and Mme. Potiphar, as the veriest child could see! But why go farther? The result was that the great church picture was closed in its box again, securely nailed, and the crowd dispersed; those on the outskirts, who had only had a passing and the briefest glimpse of this scandal, being even more indignant at the deprivation than the committee of payment over the loss of their five and fifty francs, while the good Curé Miguel was positively reduced to tears.

But the Curé Miguel is heartbroken no longer; matters have been happily arranged, and the picture now hangs in its place hiding the objectionable spot. Joseph, provided with a pair of wings, a gilded trumpet, and a belligerent expression, has become the Angel Gabriel.

Mme. Potiphar—well, there is still some doubt as to what Mme. Potiphar has become. One thing only is certain, her present draperies are most voluminously ample. She wears upon her brow a nimbus of clouds and golden stars, and the velvet of her scarlet petticoat covers about half the wall of the little church.

A PARTIAL LIST OF SNUGGLY BOOKS

ETHEL ARCHER *The Hieroglyph*
ETHEL ARCHER *Phantasy and Other Poems*
ETHEL ARCHER *The Whirlpool*
G. ALBERT AURIER *Elsewhere and Other Stories*
CHARLES BARBARA *My Lunatic Asylum*
S. HENRY BERTHOUD *Misanthropic Tales*
LÉON BLOY *The Tarantulas' Parlor and Other Unkind Tales*
ÉLÉMIR BOURGES The Twilight of the Gods
CYRIEL BUYSSE *The Aunts*
KAREL ČAPEK *Krakatit*
JAMES CHAMPAGNE *Harlem Smoke*
FÉLICIEN CHAMPSAUR *The Latin Orgy*
BRENDAN CONNELL *Unofficial History of Pi Wei*
BRENDAN CONNELL (editor)
    The Zaffre Book of Occult Fiction
BRENDAN CONNELL (editor)
    The Zinzolin Book of Occult Fiction
RAFAELA CONTRERAS *The Turquoise Ring and Other Stories*
ADOLFO COUVE *When I Think of My Missing Head*
RENÉ CREVEL *Are You All Crazy?*
QUENTIN S. CRISP *Aiaigasa*
QUENTIN S. CRISP *Graves*
LUCIE DELARUE-MARDRUS *The Last Siren and Other Stories*
LADY DILKE *The Outcast Spirit and Other Stories*
ÉDOUARD DUJARDIN *Hauntings*
BERIT ELLINGSEN *Now We Can See the Moon*
ERCKMANN-CHATRIAN *A Malediction*
ALPHONSE ESQUIROS *The Enchanted Castle*
ENRIQUE GÓMEZ CARRILLO *Sentimental Stories*
DELPHI FABRICE *Flowers of Ether*
DELPHI FABRICE *The Red Sorcerer*
DELPHI FABRICE *The Red Spider*
BENJAMIN GASTINEAU *The Reign of Satan*
EDMOND AND JULES DE GONCOURT *Manette Salomon*
REMY DE GOURMONT *From a Faraway Land*
REMY DE GOURMONT *Morose Vignettes*
GUIDO GOZZANO *Alcina and Other Stories*
LUIGI GUALDO *Narcisa and Other Stories*
GUSTAVE GUICHES *The Modesty of Sodom*
EDWARD HERON-ALLEN *The Complete Shorter Fiction*

EDWARD HERON-ALLEN *Three Ghost-Written Novels*
J.-K. HUYSMANS *The Crowds of Lourdes*
COLIN INSOLE *Valerie and Other Stories*
JUSTIN ISIS *Pleasant Tales II*
JULES JANIN *The Dead Donkey and the Guillotined Woman*
KLABUND *Spook*
GUSTAVE KAHN *The Mad King*
KLABUND *Spook*
MARIE KRYSINSKA *The Path of Amour*
BERNARD LAZARE *The Mirror of Legends*
BERNARD LAZARE *The Torch-Bearers*
JULES LERMINA *Human Life*
MAURICE LEVEL *The Shadow*
JEAN LORRAIN *Errant Vice*
JEAN LORRAIN *Masks in the Tapestry*
GEORGES DE LYS *An Idyll in Sodom*
GEORGES DE LYS *Penthesilea*
ARTHUR MACHEN *Ornaments in Jade*
PAUL MARGUERITTE *Pantomimes and Other Surreal Tales*
CAMILLE MAUCLAIR *The Frail Soul and Other Stories*
CATULLE MENDÈS *Mephistophela*
ÉPHRAÏM MIKHAËL *Halyartes and Other Poems in Prose*
LUIS DE MIRANDA *Who Killed the Poet?*
OCTAVE MIRBEAU *The 628-E8*
CHARLES MORICE *Babels, Balloons and Innocent Eyes*
GABRIEL MOUREY *Monada*
DAMIAN MURPHY *Daughters of Apostasy*
KRISTINE ONG MUSLIM *Butterfly Dream*
OSSIT *Ilse*
CHARLES NODIER *Jean Sbogar and Other Stories*
CHARLES NODIER *Outlaws and Sorrows*
HERSH DOVID NOMBERG *A Cheerful Soul and Other Stories*
PHILOTHÉE O'NEDDY *The Enchanted Ring*
GEORGES DE PEYREBRUNE *A Decadent Woman*
HÉLÈNE PICARD *Sabbat*
JEAN PRINTEMPS *Whimsical Tales*
RACHILDE *The Blood-Guzzler and Other Stories*
RACHILDE *The Princess of Darkness*
JEREMY REED *When a Girl Loves a Girl*
ADOLPHE RETTÉ *Misty Thule*
JEAN RICHEPIN *The Bull-Man and the Grasshopper*
FREDERICK ROLFE (Baron Corvo) *Amico di Sandro*

JASON ROLFE *An Archive of Human Nonsense*
ARNAUD RYKNER *The Last Train*
ROBERT SCHEFFER *Prince Narcissus and Other Stories*
ROBERT SCHEFFER *The Green Fly and Other Stories*
MARCEL SCHWOB *The Assassins and Other Stories*
MARCEL SCHWOB *Double Heart*
CHRISTIAN HEINRICH SPIESS *The Dwarf of Westerbourg*
BRIAN STABLEFORD (editor) *The Snuggly Satyricon*
BRIAN STABLEFORD (editor) *The Snuggly Satanicon*
BRIAN STABLEFORD *Spirits of the Vasty Deep*
COUNT ERIC STENBOCK *The Shadow of Death*
COUNT ERIC STENBOCK *Studies of Death*
MONTAGUE SUMMERS *The Bride of Christ and Other Fictions*
MONTAGUE SUMMERS *Six Ghost Stories*
ALICE TÉLOT *The Inn of Tears*
GILBERT-AUGUSTIN THIERRY *Reincarnation and Redemption*
DOUGLAS THOMPSON *The Fallen West*
TOADHOUSE *What Makes the Wave Break?*
LÉO TRÉZENIK *The Confession of a Madman*
LÉO TRÉZENIK *Decadent Prose Pieces*
ANNA JANE VARDILL *The Secrets of Cabalism*
RUGGERO VASARI *Raun*
ROGER VAN DE VELDE *Crackling Skulls*
ILARIE VORONCA *The Confession of a False Soul*
ILARIE VORONCA *The Key to Reality*
JANE DE LA VAUDÈRE *The Demi-Sexes and The Androgynes*
JANE DE LA VAUDÈRE
The Double Star and Other Occult Fantasies
JANE DE LA VAUDÈRE
The Mystery of Kama and Brahma's Courtesans
JANE DE LA VAUDÈRE
Three Flowers and The King of Siam's Amazon
JANE DE LA VAUDÈRE
The Witch of Ecbatana and The Virgin of Israel
AUGUSTE VILLIERS DE L'ISLE-ADAM *Isis*
RENÉE VIVIEN *Lilith's Legacy*
RENÉE VIVIEN *A Woman Appeared to Me*
ILARIE VORONCA *The Confession of a False Soul*
ILARIE VORONCA *The Key to Reality*
TERESA WILMS MONTT *In the Stillness of Marble*
TERESA WILMS MONTT *Sentimental Doubts*
KAREL VAN DE WOESTIJNE *The Dying Peasant*

Milton Keynes UK
Ingram Content Group UK Ltd.
UKHW050644260624
444769UK00004B/93